The DOGS of VENICE

ALSO BY STEVEN ROWLEY

The Guncle Abroad

The Celebrants

The Guncle

The Editor

Lily and the Octopus

The DOGS of VENICE

a novel

STEVEN ROWLEY

G. P. PUTNAM'S SONS
NEW YORK

PUTNAM
— EST. 1838 —

G. P. Putnam's Sons
Publishers Since 1838
An imprint of Penguin Random House LLC
1745 Broadway, New York, NY 10019
penguinrandomhouse.com

Book design by Nancy Resnick
Snowflake illustrations by Auguste Lange/Shutterstock
Dog silhouette by Tamim 99Graphics/Shutterstock

LIBRARY OF CONGRESS CATALOGING-IN-PUBLICATION DATA

Names: Rowley, Steven, 1971- author.
Title: The dogs of Venice : a novel / Steven Rowley.
Description: New York: G. P. Putnam's Sons, 2025.
Identifiers: LCCN 2024059736 (print) | LCCN 2024059737 (ebook) |
ISBN 9798217047604 (hardcover) | ISBN 9798217047611 (ebook)
Subjects: LCGFT: Novels.
Classification: LCC PS3618.O888 D64 2025 (print) | LCC PS3618.O888 (ebook) |
DDC 813/.6—dc23/eng/20241216
LC record available at https://lccn.loc.gov/2024059736
LC ebook record available at https://lccn.loc.gov/2024059737

Originally released as an audiobook by Audible Original, 2020.
First published in print by G. P. Putnam's Sons, 2025.

Printed in the United States of America
1st Printing

The authorized representative in the EU for product safety and compliance is
Penguin Random House Ireland, Morrison Chambers, 32 Nassau Street,
Dublin D02 YH68, Ireland, https://eu-contact.penguin.ie.

For Rob

The DOGS of VENICE

It was a trip Paul and Darren had planned together, Venice at Christmas, an idea cooked up while dining at Alice, a dark and moody Italian joint in New York's Greenwich Village. *Alice* is Italian for anchovy, one of Italy's most popular fish, something they'd learned on a previous vacation to Rome. They spent the better part of the year planning and dreaming, saving and studying, until three weeks prior, while they were admiring Bergdorf's avant-garde Christmas windows, of all things, Darren announced their marriage was over.

"This isn't working," he'd said. Convinced his husband was talking about the window display, Paul covered one eye, then turned his head sideways to see if that helped.

"I think it's the Pegasus . . . *es*." *Pegasi?* "There are too many of them." The winged creatures frolicked and kicked and were covered in mirrors like disco balls. "In Greek mythology, they sprang from the blood of Medusa when Perseus cut off her head, but I have a hard time believing that many horses could stampede out of one woman's neck." But Darren wasn't talking about the windows. By the time the departure date for their trip rolled around, he had already acquired moving boxes from the U-Haul on West 23rd.

Stunned, Paul forced himself onto the plane anyway, thinking what Darren needed was time alone; surely after a day or two he would come to his senses and maybe even make it to Italy in time for Christmas.

"Next to an empty seat. Do you always have such good luck?" asked a male flight attendant with an easy smile just after the plane's doors had closed and everyone had taken their seats. Up until that moment, Paul had his eyes trained on the aisle, thinking Darren might reconsider.

"Actually, I was supposed to take this trip to Venice with someone. But . . ." Paul couldn't bring himself to finish the sentence. Not that he needed to; heartbreak was written across his face.

The flight attendant twisted his mouth to one side but later brought him a free bottle of wine and leaned in to whisper, "My *gondolances*," causing Paul to stifle a groan. The in-flight magazine had an article about New York at Christmas, and he tore out the page with a photomontage of the city's store-window displays and used it to spit out his gum. The woman across the aisle glared at him, and Paul glared back until she returned her attention to her book.

Paul arrived in Italy via Paris, JFK to Charles de Gaulle to Marco Polo, before a water taxi ferried him briskly across the Laguna Veneta, a bay in the Adriatic Sea. Even with the extensive directions the rental company had provided, the loft Darren had booked was almost impossible to find, hidden behind an arched cutout in a crumbling wall that opened to a private cobblestone walk. Paul was so lost in the fistful of printouts he clutched tightly in one hand, studying digital photos altered with red arrows ("idiotproof," Darren had described the directions when they were first emailed), he almost wandered right into a canal when the walkway came to an unannounced end. Dusk had given way to darkness, and the canals were almost black and hard to see. It reminded him of when they last had to buy a new TV. The salesman was pushing a QLED, as it had the blackest blacks with multiple dimming zones. "Sometimes black can be too black," Paul had said at the time, and he said it again to himself now. He took a few steps back from the edge until he came to a door adorned with a coppery knocker, an ornate lion's head, and used it to rap three times.

After a minute of quiet pierced only by water lapping against the walkway, he heard footsteps and a stodgy woman whipped open the door. "*Due* people," she said when she saw only Paul standing there. In her wrap skirt with a tea towel stuck in the hem, breasts sitting right on her waist, she looked not unlike Mama Celeste from the frozen pizza commercials of his youth.

"Do people what?" asked Paul, confused, looking over his shoulder to see if he had the wrong door; this was already a mistake. Darren was the one who had brushed up on his Italian using an app while Paul had studied maps and made lists of things for them to do.

"*Due. Due*," she said, annoyed, before holding up two fingers.

"T-*two*," Paul stammered, finally understanding, and was embarrassed again anew. "Change of plans. I'm afraid you're stuck with just me." And then he added, "*Uno*," as he held up one index finger, hoping that he wasn't confusing Italian with remedial Spanish.

Mama Celeste looked at him with great skepticism, like he might have just drowned his companion in a canal; in the moment, he would consider it. "*Morto?*"

"Dead? Good heavens, no. We broke up. Divorce." Paul fumbled for his phone and the language translation app he had at the ready, as the word left a distaste in his mouth. It was the first time he'd said it aloud. "*Divorzio*." It sounded only slightly less grim in Italian.

The woman's pursed expression relaxed. Her face sagged with pity, the corners of her mouth heading south like her breasts. "*Morto* is better." Paul didn't argue as she ushered him inside, showed him the loft, and gave him a key. It was spacious and worn (but shy of dilapidated), filled with dusty books in Italian and English. On the table was a panettone and a bottle of wine with a card. The kitchen had the fanciest espresso machine he'd ever seen, and there was an oversized chair that he could lose himself in while he enjoyed his morning coffee. In short, it was exactly as Paul had dreamed. As soon as the woman left, he ripped open the card hoping it was from Darren, but alas the cake and the wine were a gift from the rental company.

Paul awoke the next morning with no message from Darren. Given that it was year's end, even his office was leaving Paul be; he was able to clear his inbox in a matter of minutes. It was when he snapped his laptop closed that he first saw the dog from the loft's picture window, which overlooked one of the city's quieter canals. The animal trotted along the narrow walkway on the far side of the water with an enviable nonchalance, its brindled scruff a perfect match for the cobblestone, a white stripe running down its nose looking extra bright in the morning sun. Unleashed and alone, the dog moved with assurance and purpose, ignoring an old man with a cane carrying a bakery box headed in the opposite direction. It scampered up and over a small footbridge, as if this were part of a daily commute, before disappearing out of sight. He then struggled with the apartment's complicated espresso machine, which hissed and spit steam and grounds. He took a few sips of an undrinkable sludge. At home, Darren had always made the coffee, as he was the earlier riser; Paul was already failing to perform simple tasks on his own. Feeling sorry for himself, he leaned in the window, waiting for the dog to return. It didn't, but something about the dog left an indelible impression.

Later, when he gathered the courage to venture into the city, he noticed several more of these street dogs; with no cars in Venice, they seemed to enjoy the run of it. None were leashed and only one he encountered was muzzled. There were very few rules regarding dogs, it seemed. Animals apparently weren't allowed in markets, but even that seemed negotiable to the Italians; while buying a bottle of Soave and a selection of local cheeses, Paul had witnessed a corgi patiently waiting for its owner by the checkout and no one appeared to mind. Outside another shop in the Campo Santa Margherita, a small pooch demanded the complete attention of a security guard, who was more than happy to oblige. These dogs seemed to rule the roost. But there was something about *his* dog's shabby confidence, the one that had passed his apartment, that stirred an awakening in Paul. It was so comfortable in its own skin and possessed such command; he could easily picture the dog waiting nightly in an alley behind a sleepy bistro for the chef to reveal from under a cloche a leftover bone from the kitchen's special osso buco. Before the dog was a distant memory, Paul thought, *That's who I want to be.*

He prized the tranquil mornings most, when he would sit in the loft's window, although the espresso machine continued to be challenging. This morning it offered only drips and dribbles, a cruel taunt, since he was in desperate need of caffeine. "We are *not* compatible," he said out loud, but it was unclear if he was speaking to the machine or his ex. A quick search online said the grounds may be too fine. Undeterred, he licked the inside of the cappuccino cup, getting every drop he could, then washed it down with a slice of the panettone, which was dry like last night's wine. Instinctively he knew this was cheating. Anyone can be alone behind closed doors; the goal was to be comfortable by himself in a *caffè* under the gaze of watchful eyes. Still, he reasoned, these mornings were a start and gave him something to build on, and he was forgiving of himself. He was brittle still, and forlorn, delighted only in spite of himself by the gauzy December light that made him feel like he'd stepped into a Renaissance artist's paint box, and the occasional gondolier in traditional Venetian stripes rowing by. And it wasn't like he hadn't ventured outside. He'd spent a whole day touring Venice on foot, getting blissfully lost and finding his way again, looking down at the beautiful blue-green waters that filled an endless maze of canals and then up for signs pointing to familiar landmarks like the Piazza San Marco or the Ponte di Rialto—sometimes the only clues to guide him home. And Christmas was a magical time, especially in Piazza San Marco, which he'd heard dubbed "Europe's living room." And it was decked out appropriately! Thousands of lights dripped from the porticoes and the Christmas tree square in the center was glorious. This year's tree was traditional, but he overheard someone remark that every year the tree was different, and sometimes surprisingly modern. An app on his phone informed him he'd averaged nineteen thousand steps that first day (to his barking feet it felt like more). Besides, it was clear what he was doing. He was waiting for the dog to return.

At lunchtime, and with no sign of his four-legged friend, Paul picked at leftover ravioli from his meal the night before. He'd stumbled on a treasure, Osteria alle Testiere, and had felt confident as he sat down for his meal. But after three bites he'd succumbed to relentless self-consciousness and asked for the rest of his food to go. Later, he put aside a prawn and a bit of ravioli and placed them on a saucer, which he then set outside on the edge of the walkway close to a wall. If nothing else, he hoped it would lure the dog back this way. He returned to his window to let the bait do its work, and while he waited, wrote a few thoughts on the trip in his journal. Already he'd experienced magnificent things—art and history and ancient architecture, cathedrals and basilicas. New York had these things, too (although they were slightly less ancient), but he hardly noticed them anymore, consumed as he was by life's daily drudgery. Sights became obstacles drawing crowds that were difficult to navigate around. Here, he had become an expert at lingering near tour groups without joining them, eavesdropping on facts that piqued his interest before detaching and scuttling away. It was how he felt about society as a whole, always on the outside of it and never quite part of the group, one of the reasons why he'd always valued his marriage; he found comfort in partnership, even when that union was, apparently, a sham. But he loved learning things, so he listened; an enduring interest in the world made him feel slightly less like a loner. There were four hundred seventeen bridges in Venice, but seventy-two of them were private. There were three hundred fifty or so gondolas, but more than four hundred *gondolieri*, so some of them had to share. Venice was sinking at the rate of one, maybe two, millimeters a year, which didn't sound like much, but the city was already built on a precarious foundation. Each guide would offer such facts before raising a closed umbrella or bright-colored cap to signal their group. The tour would then follow the guide as they offered more numbers and figures and stats, and Paul would continue alone.

It wasn't like anything these tours could offer would distract him from some telling numbers of his own; Paul made a list in his journal. While he was *four thousand* miles from home, his *one* husband was moving out. When he returned to their *third*-floor Gramercy Park apartment, *scores* of things would be gone. *Hundreds* of arguments, *dozens* of holidays, *fifteen* birthdays, *two thousand seven hundred fifty-five* "good night"s. Paul, it seemed, was sinking much faster than Venice—he, too, was on shifting ground. Until he recognized in a street dog the confidence he lacked in himself, and the dog became his central fascination. He'd come to Venice not to observe, but to grow—he'd written as much on the plane over Newfoundland. He figured the dog could be a teacher, as Paul had much to learn. Alas, it was apparently uninterested in prawns.

He thought of the dog all afternoon at the Guggenheim, where Peggy, niece of Solomon, was buried next to her fourteen Lhasa apsos in the hope that they would join her in the afterlife. Paul rented an audio tour to quell his nerves—it was okay not to have someone to talk to when listening to a headset. Peggy was, the tour said, unparalleled as a collector and curator; highlights included Picassos and Dalís and Pollocks. But Paul was drawn outdoors, where a simple plaque marked the resting place of her beloved Lhasa apsos: Cappucino, Pegeen, Peacock, Toro, Foglia, Madam Butterfly, Baby, Emily, White Angel, Sir Herbert, Sable, Gypsy, Hong Kong, and Cellida. He wondered if he should give his dog a name, the one he'd seen and hoped to see again, but a name suggested a kind of ownership, and Paul knew what his fascination meant: It was the dog, in fact, who owned him. Paul decided to think of the animal simply as the Dog.

When he returned to the loft to bandage a blister, Mama Celeste was waiting for him holding the saucer, eyeing suspiciously his limp. "*Cos'è questo?*" she asked, shoving the saucer in his face. The ravioli was gone, and most of the prawn.

"I'm sorry," Paul replied, stunned. He knew from her tone he was in trouble. "I left that out for the dog." He took the saucer from her sheepishly. "Do you know the dog that passes by here?" He fumbled for his phone with his free hand. "*Cane?*"

"*Non sono ammessi cani.*" Mama Celeste grabbed a nearby broom and made a shooing motion. "No dogs allow." She then dived into a monologue in Italian, and Paul took that as his cue to duck away. After he bandaged his foot, he waited until she returned to her own apartment to venture out again.

In line to climb the Campanile di San Marco to watch the sunset from the bell tower's observatory, he spotted the Dog a second time. He wasn't certain at first, but the white stripe on its snout gave the Dog's identity away; up close it was clear he was male. He bustled past Paul with the same cocky air as before, expertly navigating his way through the throng of tourists, pausing only to side-eye a chorus in robes singing hymns. Paul's heart beat faster and his whole body constricted, the way it had long ago when he had unexpectedly seen Darren in Bryant Park dining with another man before they'd made their relationship exclusive.

"*Mi scusi,*" he said to the elderly gentleman behind him, who was smoking some sort of European cigarillo. He bolted from the line to chase after the Dog, who was already giving him the slip. His canine friend kept a serious-minded pace toward his destination—the café tables on the far side of the flagpoles that marked the entrance to the piazza. Paul kept a distance he thought would be safe, knowing an animal could change course on a dime; he desperately didn't want to lose him. He wished to get close to, but not interfere with, the Dog's grift; he was there to observe. People enjoying their early dinners—Americans mostly, always concerned with food, and also some Japanese—tossed bits of pastry or bread, or a bite of prosciutto from a sandwich. Paul marveled at the scam. It worked because the Dog never begged, never showed much in the way of interest (or gratitude), and didn't stick around for more than he was offered. It was like he was happy to connect, but he didn't expect connect*ion*, and he worked the tables efficiently, tolerating a few scratches behind the ears before moving on, weaving under the holiday wreaths that hung from the archways framing the storefronts like none of this had happened.

That was Paul's mistake, at least according to Darren; he had always expected too much.

He'd even said this to Paul when they were first dating, the accusation dripping with a displeasure that didn't fully register with Paul until a good while later. Perhaps their pairing should have been capped after a few dates, before they consented to a relationship. Or at most a seasonal fling, a warm body with which to get through the winter, if an expiration date was so obvious. But Paul had pushed, wanting more, as he always did, eager to give away the key to his heart. And why not? He thought they enjoyed each other's company. When Darren accepted his proposal, he actually seemed to delight in planning their wedding, and for a while things were good. Paul asked him in the fizzled tail of one of their fiery arguments, why, why, if he was unhappy, did he say yes? Darren answered that he had hoped marriage would calm Paul's neuroses, that if Paul could accept that they were together, their union legally sanctioned by the state, he would eventually hold Darren a little less tight. But having someone made Paul *more* afraid of losing them, not less; in their therapist's office Darren accused Paul of wanting a conjoined twin more than a husband, and the marriage was over in less than five years. College for each of them, including their graduate degrees, had been longer.

Paul waved at the Dog, as if he might recognize him (which of course he did not), then pursued the Dog through the archways, pushing through a family who had stopped to gawk at pastries. Sensing a chase, the Dog picked up his pace until both of them were at a full sprint, as if he knew what Paul did—a James Bond movie with Daniel Craig had been filmed in the very same spot. The Dog had an easier time of it than Paul; he was more nimble, able to pivot and dodge. His focus was singular—getting away. Paul was slowed by apologizing, by caring enough not to offend, to appear rational in the throes of an obsession that was anything but. When he burst out of the piazza by the waterfront, he caught a glimpse of the Dog running in the distance before ducking into an alley. By the time Paul reached the alley, he was gone.

Paul stopped along the waterfront to catch his breath, doubling over to place his hands on his knees. He should start running again, he thought, like he had in college; he was too young to be this winded. When he was able to stand he stared at the bay, almost surprised to find it in front of him, and watched as the boats came and went from Murano. He hated that Darren was right. When Paul was lucky enough to get something he liked, he always stayed for more. He couldn't help it; it was how he was built—which was what made the Dog such an enigma; how could any creature find satisfaction in meaningless interactions and scraps? But the world was not like that, not like him. The world was much more like the Dog. People nowadays were callous, inattentive, fed on diets of apps and devices that were constantly changing and offering something new. He knew he had to learn to at least *appear* nonchalant; his future happiness depended on it. If he could only corner his teacher.

As he watched the gulls glide over the gondolas docked for the night, pondering how a stray dog could be better suited for the world than he, a portly tour guide's loud whistling caught his attention as the man casually counted the day's tips. Dressed in an oversized cable-knit sweater that made him seem even rounder, he looked like the kind of man Bob Hoskins used to play in films—gruff, but amiable underneath. Paul focused on the gondolas so he wouldn't appear to be lurking, and waited for the man to finish his count before speaking.

"*Mi scusi.* May I ask you a question?" Paul asked. All the guides spoke English—perhaps not perfectly, but better than Mama Celeste.

"But of course!" The man's tone was enthusiastic, as if he were eager to answer; he checked his watch nonetheless. By day he played a character, the jovial Italian—most of the guides and *gondolieri* did, like they were seconds away from singing. But in the last ribbon of daylight, it was clear this man was eager to hang up his cap.

"The dogs I see running around the city. The street dogs." Paul realized in his effort to make this quick, he hadn't proffered much of a question. He scrambled to follow up. "Do they belong to anyone? Residents?"

The man was bald with a salt-and-pepper beard and wore a scarf tied around his neck. He looked up and down the waterfront, perhaps for an example of one of these dogs, but it was nearing dinner and they no doubt had retreated for food. "There is a saint," he began. "San Rocco? Saint Roch, in English, yes? The patron saint of dogs, among other things—the falsely accused, and bachelors. He's very important to Venice. A dog saved San Rocco when he was suffering by bringing him bread and licking his wounds. Tomorrow you visit the Chiesa di San Rocco, the Church of Saint Roch. There you will learn more." He pointed west and a little bit north, a direction Paul assumed led to the church. "Dogs, they are part of the city of Venice. Do they belong? They are . . . *domesticated.* That is the word? A few wander the city. Rome has cats, Venice has dogs. Me? I have two cats, but I prefer Venezia to Roma." He shrugged—*What are you going to do?*—then tucked his money in a shocking neon waist bag, concealed by his sweater, that made him look like he was only a pair of leg warmers shy of heading to do aerobics at the gym.

"I've seen the cats in Rome," Paul said, and he had. He and Darren had traveled there two summers ago, after a week on the Italian coast. They'd sought out a cat sanctuary known as the Torre Argentina after hearing a profile on the women who ran it on NPR's *Weekend Edition.* Hundreds of cats roamed the ruins where Caesar was murdered, sunbathing on ancient pillars and steps. Darren had made a joke at the time: No wonder cats liked it there given its history; dogs, who valued loyalty, would never assemble in a place of betrayal. Paul reached into his pocket for euros and handed the guide several coins.

"*Grazie,*" the man said, happily accepting his tip. Then he repeated, "Chiesa di San Rocco," and gave Paul a thumbs-up.

Alone again, Paul strolled the waterfront with this new information, wondering if the Dog had a family or if all of

Venice was his home. Certainly cats could be feral; it wasn't just Rome that had those. But dogs? They seemed, like him, more dependent. He weaved through the crowds that gathered to watch the last of the sun color the waters that fed the Grand Canal, then turned to look above the city's rooftops. He could just make out the tip of the bell tower, but it was too late to rejoin the queue for the observatory. He could try again tomorrow. Besides, he was content where he was. Before, he'd enjoyed the anonymity this strange city offered him, reasoning he could be anyone and others would not judge. But in this moment he took comfort in the people around him, letting these strangers ease the aching loneliness that hid underneath a facade.

The patron saint of dogs, bachelors, and the falsely accused, Paul thought. How were these things assigned? Randomly upon canonization? Did they pick slips of paper from a bowl? Peter, you get premature baldness, cabbage, and sloths. John? Sandwich cookies with double the filling, dolphins, and adults who can't tell time. His own name came from Paul the Apostle; his mother's love of the Church confirmed that. But he had no earthly clue of what Paul was the patron saint. Popping bubble wrap? Jorts? Men who don't like canned peas? Still, even in the midst of these absurd thoughts, Paul could see a connection, a certain wisdom, in the assignments to San Rocco, and it made him feel less alone. Perhaps his new bachelordom was why he felt an affinity for this dog, or how he felt falsely accused by his own husband of being so needy. *Ex-husband.* With Darren failing to materialize, it seemed all over but the paperwork. On his phone Paul made a note: *Chiesa di San Rocco.* He felt a pressing need to know more about Saint Roch, and the church would certainly be something to see. He wanted to know everything about this saint that was looking out for him.

At nine Paul dressed for dinner and headed out for a late meal. Mama Celeste was standing guard outside the building, ready to chase any dogs away. He wished she wouldn't do that, but didn't know how to get her to lessen her grip on her broom.

"*Buonasera*," Paul said to be friendly.

The woman looked at her watch, and pursed her lips as if to keep from saying what was clearly written across her face—no good ever came from someone leaving the house this late.

"La Zucca," Paul said, referencing the popular bistro, which was difficult to get into at any more reasonable hour. But since *zucca* also meant "pumpkin," this only confused Mama Celeste. She looked at him with a mixture of pity and scorn, as if this conversation were impolite.

La Zucca earned raves in his guidebook, but a proper meal alone was still his Everest, especially one as formal as dinner. He had never had much interest in animal meat other than fish, and the restaurant's largely vegetarian menu appealed to him. Over the course of their relationship, Darren's strict vegetarian cooking had pushed him away from meat even more. In defiance of his ex, he thought about a meaty *ragù*, thinking it might even be a better offering for the Dog. But there was no point in losing himself to spite someone else. Besides, the night already felt full of promise, as if he were about to settle an old score.

"How are you going to travel by yourself? You can't even eat lunch unescorted," Darren had said when Paul announced he was still taking their trip. And there was plenty of truth to his husband's observation; Paul had always felt self-conscious alone. *But look at me now*, he thought, making his way to a restaurant clear on the other side of the world. Perhaps Paul was the saint of proving doubters wrong, if only he could get through tonight's meal. If nothing else, he was looking forward to ordering as he pleased (Darren always wanted to share) and a menu that didn't require his phone's constant translating, wondering if unfamiliar Italian words were types of cheeses or meats.

The winter air was crisp, pleasant. Paul wore a scarf he'd purchased in one of the local boutiques, tied in the fashion the shopgirl had shown him; it made him feel very Italian. With his curls swooped under a knit cap and his quilted coat, he thought he looked rather Italian, too, but like a fisherman, perhaps, from Cinque Terre. He searched for the Dog as he wove through the streets to warn him of Mama Celeste and her broom, wondering the whole time if anyone, even the natives, ever learned their way around. He'd overheard a shopkeeper mention to a tourist that the population of Venice had been cut in half over the last fifty years, which, despite the throngs of holiday tourists that made the city feel swollen, Paul had no reason to believe was untrue. Residents were fed up with the foreigners, perhaps, or the difficult way of life. Yet the Dog seemed somehow to thrive, so the city was still suitable for some.

He crossed over the Grand Canal, feeling lost, until he stumbled upon a statue he recognized. After several more rights, three lefts, a handful of narrow bridges over the smaller waterways, and a quick consultation with his phone, he found the restaurant. Lit with soft moonlight, it took on the aura of a Hollywood film set.

"*Buonasera*," he said to the host, rubbing his hands in the warmth of the small *osteria*. "Reservation for Hafner." Calling his Italian "conversational" would be generous, but there was no reason for him to stress—in a restaurant such as this, most everyone spoke English.

La Zucca was outfitted with homey wood-paneled walls with an inviting wine collection lining the back; the air smelled of butter and sage. The atmosphere was warm, exotic in the way that Europe feels different from America, but comfortable and familiar, too, like a distant relative's home, filled with voices that melted into an ambient din. Paul was seated alone at a table for two (*Get back on the horse*, he thought), the chair opposite him embarrassingly the lone empty seat in the place. He had come prepared with a paperback copy of some thriller he'd picked up at the airport, as well as a long article from *The New Yorker* he'd downloaded on his phone. It was important, he felt, to acclimate; if he was going to at least get as far as a fourth bite tonight, he couldn't rely on his crutches up front. A handsome waiter offered him bread. His thick, dark hair was peppered with premature salt, and his eyes were deep-set and brown; they paired well with a ready smile. His looks made Paul so nervous he ordered two dishes, the tagliatelle with artichokes and pecorino, and a zucchini lasagna (which the waiter called *indimenticabile*), along with a *quartino* of wine. Paul hoped two entrées would help mask the fact that he was one, saving him face in front of the staff. When the waiter left, Paul dragged his bread through olive oil, cursing himself for being so awkward.

When his dinner arrived, Paul concentrated on his food and didn't look at his paperback once. It was, he imagined, what the Dog would have done. The tagliatelle belied its simple ingredients, the cheese shaved to perfection so that it stood up to the dish and the artichokes browned to offset their briny flavor. The lasagna was layered with three sauces, each failing to disappoint. The waiter was right—it was unforgettable. He was amazed at how different food tasted when it was the sole focus, absent the distraction of conversation. Their arguments had often centered around Paul's faults, but Darren was not without his own. Barreling through a meal like it was a hundred yard dash and talking with his mouth full were but two. The looks Paul would get when Darren was finished and his own plate hardly touched were withering. But now Paul lingered in the candlelight, savoring each forkful with an appreciation for both ingredient and technique, unearthing the china pattern on the restaurant's dishes with the slow precision of an archaeologist. He wrapped some of the lasagna in a napkin for the Dog and tucked it in his coat pocket. When he took his last bite and set down the fork, Paul was surprised to see there were empty seats all around him.

"Your meal was good, yes?" It was the handsome waiter, smoking a cigarette beside the *osteria*'s front door. Paul stood and breathed in the night air with its hint of tobacco, in no hurry to return to his loft, stealing glances when he could at the young man's profile and his strong aquiline nose.

"*Meals*," Paul replied, emphasizing the plural and humbling himself a bit. He had been basking in the triumph of his evening and thought it better to pierce his success with a joke before someone else could step forth with a sharper barb.

They both laughed, much to Paul's relief.

"In Venice alone?" the waiter asked, his stare intense, cutting right to Paul's deepest insecurity. It may have been the shadows, but Paul swore the man's scruff had darkened since he'd first arrived at the table with bread. He was overcome with a sudden desire to touch it, rub it like sandpaper across his bare skin just to see what it felt like; Darren's face had always been boyish and smooth.

"Sadly." Paul shrugged before looking down at his shoes, scuffed from walking the city. Dining alone had made Paul a tourist attraction unto himself.

"Not sad for me." The waiter smiled, giving Paul a sudden appreciation for truth. "I like your *sciarpa*. Very Italian."

It took Paul a moment to follow, but then he loosened the scarf around his neck, making it easier to breathe. "My scarf?"

"*Sciarpa*, yes. I have one just like." The waiter pulled his own scarf out of his back pocket; it was nothing like Paul's.

"Do you know your way at night? Streets in Venice are full of dark. Dark that can be *too* dark."

"That's what I always say," Paul agreed, looking up at the half-moon and suddenly wishing it were full. The city's gloomy emptiness at this late hour made it infinitely more menacing. In New York the streets were wide and alive, never empty of cars, which flew like hail at all hours, and the city always gave off light. A QLED TV would be a waste in Manhattan, as it was never dark enough to allow for true black.

"I walk with you." The waiter dropped the butt of his cigarette and crushed it out with his foot.

"What, right now?"

The waiter looked confused. "Yes. I finish for the night. You? Or would you like a third meal?"

It was all so forward it took Paul by surprise and he blushed at the suggestion he wasn't yet sated. "Paul," he said, offering his hand, not knowing what else to say.

The waiter took Paul's hand and shook it without breaking his gaze. "Nicola." His hand was surprisingly warm, as if he'd just served a hot dish. "After you."

Together they walked through the winding streets, talking the whole way about Italy, about Venice, Nicola the one tour guide Paul didn't shy away from, and it felt good not to just eavesdrop but to actually listen. And be able to offer his own insights in return.

"Venice is more than *cento isole* . . . islands," Nicola offered.

"*Cento.* One hundred?"

"*Sì.* Many, many bridges to connect them all."

In that moment, Paul was a bridge, yearning to connect; he just didn't want to be walked over. "I heard Venice is shrinking," he said.

"Sinking," Nicola said, correcting him.

"That, too." And indeed the ground felt like it was shifting under his feet. "But I mean, fewer people."

"Ah," Nicola said. "Yes, people leave."

It was a punch to Paul's full stomach. He stared at his companion, wondering if he had any idea how profound his simple observations were. *People leave.* Darren had left. His father, when Paul was young. It was just that straightforward and matter-of-fact.

"Venice is . . . very soft, romantic," Nicola continued. "But look close. She is a hard way of life. Balance is difficult to find."

This resonated with Paul on two levels. First, there was a slight vertiginous feeling that followed you when constantly walking along narrow canals. Second, no fairy-tale setting like Venice holds up under a microscope. "I have a theory that people leave their houses for the market one morning and are never able to find their way back. Eventually they just think, *To hell with it,* and settle somewhere else."

"To hell with it." Nicola smirked. "I like this theory."

"You know. Other cities, with luxuries like transportation and grids and street signs." According to Paul's guidebook even the postmen in Venice didn't *really* know their routes and had to rely on landmarks and shops for bearings. To Paul, this made the Dog's phlegmatic gallivanting all the more impressive.

Nicola leaned into Paul so that their shoulders touched, and he laughed. His breath smelled like cigarettes, but also sweet like a ricotta filling. "I have no idea where is my house."

Paul smirked. "Then it's a good thing we're headed to mine." If the Italians could be this direct, so could he. He braced himself for rejection, Nicola's slamming on the brakes, but the waiter didn't so much as flinch.

They crossed the Grand Canal at the Ponte dell'Accademia, farther down than the Rialto. They stopped at the bridge's center, and without the market stalls that lined the larger bridge, they were able to look out in the direction of the bay. They stood in silence.

It was Nicola who spoke first. "Do you like being alone?"

"I have to. There is no one else here."

"I am here," Nicola said, playfully nudging Paul's shoulder.

"I'm getting used to it. Being alone. It's new for me."

"The city is your friend."

Paul smiled bashfully.

"Does this scare you?" Nicola asked.

The question took Paul by surprise. *Scare* wasn't the right word, even if being alone unnerved him. He shook his head no.

"What does, then?"

Paul didn't understand this line of questioning. Did he seem afraid? Or was this Nicola shirking the banal in favor of something deeper, in the way Americans seldom did? The real answer was that Paul was scared he'd reached the age where life stopped giving you things and started taking away. But instead he said, "Long silences. You?"

"People who are not themselves," Nicola said, and Paul thought it was a perfect answer. They watched as a wooden motorboat cruised under the bridge.

"Do you know the story of the scorpion and the frog?" Paul asked. "Fable, I guess, is more accurate."

They both leaned on the bridge so that their hands overlapped. Nicola's skin was much tanner than his, with a bit of dark hair below his knuckles. "Scorpion . . . *Scorpione*. It stings?"

"Exactly. A scorpion and a frog meet on the bank of a stream and the scorpion asks the frog to carry him across on its back. The frog asks, 'How do I know you won't sting me?' And the scorpion replies, 'Because if I do, I will die, too.'"

Nicola nods his understanding, *They will both sink*, and looks at Paul to continue.

"The frog is satisfied, and so they set out, the scorpion on the frog's back. But midstream the scorpion stings the frog."

"Why?" Nicola utters, as if shocked.

"The frog feels the onset of paralysis." Paul gasps, then freezes up to demonstrate, in case the word doesn't translate. "He starts to sink. They are both going to drown. The frog has just enough time to ask, 'Why?'" He points to Nicola to show he asked the right question. "And the scorpion replies, 'Because it's my nature . . .'"

"And they drown?"

"They drown."

"*È la mia natura.*"

"'Because it's my nature,'" Paul repeated. "I don't know what made me think of that," he added, but he did know. Sometimes even when people are themselves, you should still be afraid.

"In Venezia, you cross many streams. Always can be dangerous." Again, Nicola's stripped-down English came across as profound.

"We are midstream right now," Paul agreed.

"But we don't need frog."

Paul laughed. "No. Not when we have this bridge."

"Are you afraid *I* sting?" Nicola asked.

Paul looked into his new friend's brown eyes. All these questions about being afraid. "No," he replied, and he wasn't.

As they walked the narrow street in front of his loft, Paul glanced at where the saucer had been before Mama Celeste intervened. There was a pang in his heart, like there was no longer a way for him to track the Dog's whereabouts. His building's courtyard was empty, and he was grateful for the privacy. Paul could only imagine the choice words in Italian his landlord might share when he brought home a stranger, let alone one of the same sex. He then laughed, imagining being cockblocked by Mama Celeste.

"What is funny?" Nicola asked.

"The lock sticks," Paul said after he fumbled with his key, although it wasn't the least bit amusing. Still, Nicola gave it a try.

"The air is damp," the Italian offered as explanation. Nicola threw himself against the door once and then twice, then gave it a good tug back toward them before trying the key again. This time it worked. "Voilà," he said, which was French.

Inside, Paul flipped on the lights and slipped off his shoes. "Make yourself comfortable," he told Nicola as he discreetly placed the leftover lasagna in the fridge. He opened a bottle of Sangiovese he'd bought the night he arrived and poured them each a glass. They talked and drank, and the pull between them was palpable, something Paul hadn't experienced for a long time. They stood in the open picture window, leaning on the balustrade, the cold air and the company making him feel absolutely electric. Nicola said he preferred winter in Venice, as the city was overrun with cruise ships in summer and the canals had an unpleasant smell. He spoke in more detail about living in Italy, about what had drawn him to Venice and what he knew would eventually drive him away. He wanted to be an artist, he confided, but the tourists were not interested in art, just trinkets that were largely imported from the East.

"Tourists, they have no taste," Nicola explained.

"I brought you home with me," Paul teased. "Are you saying I have no taste?"

"For every rule there is an exception," Nicola said, and, as they spoke, Paul topped off their glasses, the wine thoroughly warming their insides. "Beside, I bring myself here." Paul could allow his confidence to be knocked down a peg or two, but having a sense of Nicola, the Italian could simply mean that he walked on his own two feet.

Paul came clean about his obsession, describing the Dog in detail, down to the white stripe on his snout; he remained, however, tight-lipped about why his imagination was so captured. He pointed at the walkway where the saucer had been, the spot where he'd first noticed the creature. He hoped his guest might have seen him around, be able to offer a clue as to his regular haunts, but Nicola confessed he did not know of such a dog. He took Paul's wineglass and set it on the side table next to his own; while shorter than Paul by two inches, he took charge by putting his hands around the American's waist. Paul mumbled nervously, something about an exhibit he'd seen at the Guggenheim, hoping it would spark a connection, get them to talk more about art. But the connection was already sparked and Nicola rested a finger on Paul's lips until he fell quiet, and then replaced that finger with a kiss, to which Paul responded with a hiccup.

Nicola immediately recoiled, and Paul shot up a finger as he said a silent, desperate prayer to the patron saint of ridding one of hiccups—whomever that might be—and for once in his life his prayers were answered. Miraculously that particular saint was also assigned sex with strangers. This time Paul leaned in, and passion took over again.

Paul hadn't kissed anyone since Darren, at least not anyone he could recall. There had been a drunken night at a bar immediately after Darren had broken things off, a misguided attempt to go home with someone to get it over with, put some sort of punctuation on the end of their marriage; *this isn't working*, Darren's words, ran back and forth through his head. When Paul awoke with a pounding hangover, the events of the night had been a haze. If he had made out with someone, certainly it was nothing like this, two strangers cast in the long glow of moonlight on the other side of the world. Paul leaned into his guest for fear the shock of the moment might cause him to fall backward over the railing. Yet he quickly found his sea legs and they kissed hungrily, as if starving, their mouths tasting faintly like dark cherries from the wine.

Eventually, Paul pulled his guest toward the ladder that led to the sleeping platform. It was amazing how a new body could feel so different, firm where Darren was soft, hairy where his ex was smooth. It was both more exciting and less; he didn't know the nooks, the smells, how his own body would feel in comparison, the places he would fit, but he was in the moment, eager to discover it all. They climbed the ladder, Nicola first, pausing momentarily, looking not unlike koala bears hanging from eucalyptus trees, as they used their spare hands to unbutton their shirts before pulling themselves up to the bed.

Since there wasn't enough headspace to stand upright, Nicola pushed Paul onto the mattress, pinning his arms above his head. He was rough but gentle, assertive but not menacing, sensing correctly that Paul needed someone to take charge. Paul wanted to ask if he did this often, preyed on men dining alone. But an answer—any answer—would only ruin it. Certainly the Dog wouldn't ask a potential mate if they came to this alley often. No, they would just hump. So Paul followed suit, allowing Nicola to lash his belt around Paul's wrists, slipping it through the buckle, then wrapping the leather around his own fist, pulling it tight. Paul was now like a dog from New York and not Venice—*leashed.* With his right hand, Nicola slowly teased open Paul's pants. Exposed and obviously excited, Paul gave way to the enormous emotional comfort of another's body weight on top of him. Sex with this stranger had to be like wandering Venice: He could look up, he could look down, but there were too many corners to map far ahead. To be like the Dog, he had to remain in the moment.

Paul woke with a start, and the unnerving feeling of a shadowy figure lurking over him; he could just make out Nicola already half dressed. "It's you," he said, as if vaguely recalling a dream.

"It's me," Nicola replied while zipping his pants before working his belt through the loops. Paul felt his bare wrists, surprised not to find the belt there.

"You won't stay?"

"No," Nicola replied, soft but firm.

"Stay," Paul cajoled. "In the morning I'll make us espresso." He then winced when he remembered the espresso machine was his nemesis, but maybe the coffee gods would smile on him now that he'd proven himself less pathetic. "We'll sit by the window." The loft hadn't felt empty before, when it was just him, but Paul knew it would feel dreadfully bare once his guest left. He was eager to invite someone into his routine.

Nicola said nothing, but smiled as he slid on his shoes.

"There's cake, and maybe some cheese." Paul struggled in his haze to remember. Whatever was in his fridge, they wouldn't starve. He could even run out for some fruit if need be. "Perhaps we'll see the Dog from the window."

"I have to get home."

"You can't find your home. Remember?" Paul pulled Nicola by the arm toward the bed, imploring him to climb back in.

Nicola smiled, confirmation that he remembered the joke.

"Why do you have to go?" Paul could feel it bubbling to the surface, the desperation that had killed his marriage. It had left him for a few hours, but like a boomerang it came whipping back. He glanced toward the window for his mentor, hoping to see the Dog's shadow in the moonlight, amplified in the night like a monster.

"Because," Nicola said, "I have a girlfriend."

Paul sat upright, leaning back against the headboard. *A girlfriend?* If he'd said anything else, Paul could have understood, at least chalked it up to the ambiguity in translation. But *girlfriend* was pretty universal, pretty unambiguous. He felt angry, as if Nicola had been dishonest. "Is this what you do? Smoke cigarettes in the night and hustle wounded tourists?"

"What is 'hustle'?"

Paul grew angrier still. Nicola's English seemed to take leave of him when convenient. "Take advantage of."

Nicola shrugged. "Is that what I did?" He seemed amused, backlit in the ambient light.

"Then why are you here?"

Nicola stopped, as if he hadn't really thought about it. As if following Paul home had been the most natural thing in the world. He leaned down and kissed Paul on the forehead, running his fingers through his hair.

Paul gave him one last look, desperate for an explanation.

Nicola sighed. "*È la mia natura.*"

Alone when the sun rose, Paul wrapped a blanket around his naked body and headed straight for the window in hopes of seeing the Dog. To the left he saw three small motorboats tethered to their doorways, two with tarps over their seats.

A couple walked hand in hand over the narrow footbridge, and there was the faint echo of laughter. But no Dog. To the right, a blue-and-white-striped barber pole leaned like the Tower of Pisa out of the murky canal. The morning sun burned, reflecting off the canal's easy ripples, diamonds of light spilling across blue velvet that made him squint. With no sign of the Dog in that direction either, he raised his arm to shield his eyes and withdrew into the apartment. It was Christmas Eve.

He gave the espresso machine his best *Don't fuck with me* look as he took a deep breath and filled it anew with beans. It didn't help that the buttons and dials were labeled in Italian, but the illustrations of cup sizes and thermometers with different temperatures shaded in made it seem more or less idiotproof, and the word *pressione* surely had to mean "pressure." He checked everything one last time, and when he flipped the switch, much to his relief, the grinder whirred to life.

"How is divorce like espresso?" his brother had asked when Paul called him before he left to wish him a Merry Christmas. His brother had been through a divorce the previous year. The answer: *Both are bitter and expensive.*

Paul shook his head as he tamped the grounds and carefully locked in the portafilter. He pressed the button to pull a shot and . . . nothing. He pressed it again. This time the machine beeped three times before belching steam. Paul jumped back to avoid getting injured (he'd been burned by this contraption enough) and the appliance rattled and shook in response, throwing a little tantrum. When it finished, it emitted a high-pitched beep that continued uninterrupted until he unplugged the machine in defeat. His face ran hot with failure, and he brought his fist down on the lid three times in frustration; fortunately it stayed in one piece.

He sat, agitated and adrift. What he'd thought would be a giant leap forward, a casual encounter with a handsome stranger, had actually set him reeling back. He deserved the connection, had every right to experience great sex. So why did he feel so aimless and more alone than ever? He paced in the apartment; with the furniture, it only allowed him five steps in either direction. He stared at the espresso machine, but couldn't make himself climb back on that horse. He looked in the fridge. There was an emptiness inside him that food would not fill. He cursed Darren for doing this to him, abandoning him to undertake this trip alone. They should have been off for a breakfast together, a coffee and croissant in true Venetian style, before undertaking a leisurely, romantic day. Instead he was spiraling, swathed in a blanket like it was some sort of cocoon, except what emerged would never be beautiful.

In desperate need of caffeine, Paul threw on his clothes

from the night before. Knowing the bites of lasagna he'd saved would not stay appetizing in his pocket, he wrapped cubes of cheese in a paper towel to bribe the Dog if he found him. Instead of walking his usual route toward Piazza San Marco (he wasn't ready to face throngs of tourists in jovial holiday moods), he headed in the opposite direction, into Castello, in hopes of finding more locals and perhaps the Dog's owner. The buildings in this more-residential neighborhood were mostly brick and rust-colored stucco, the odd one a shade of marigold. The rooflines had a more uniform aesthetic, like they were made of perfectly cleaved flowerpots.

He paused in a small *caffè*, desperate for a large, black, American-style coffee to give him the jolt he needed for his search. The barista was deep in a heated argument with two brutish men whose jackets were caked with dirt. Paul was definitely off the beaten path; there wasn't a tourist around. The men argued loudly about something he assumed to be sports or politics—two things that universally provoked men's ire—and, his brain still foggy, he grew increasingly intimidated. There was something about not being able to understand conversation that made one feel particularly forsaken. He had all but turned to leave when the barista finally acknowledged him with a grunt. Nervous, Paul's Italian failed him, but he pleaded in English for a large, black coffee or the type of obnoxious latte one might get at Starbucks—

a Star*bucket*, if you will. He was somehow served a cup of steamed milk. Maybe in his delirious state he had ordered it, maybe he hadn't, maybe the men in this place were trying to hassle him, move him along from their turf. Paul threw down a few coins, muttering, "*Grazie*," hoping his dog didn't belong to one of these thugs. He left like he'd just been mugged.

Plenty of mutts were about in the morning sun, but not a single one looked familiar. Here they were largely ignored by locals, but appeared friendly nonetheless; a few came right up to Paul and he used the last of his energy to pet them. The dogs came in a variety of colors and trims, mostly medium in size, and all had a similar air as the object of his fascination, but not quite the confidence to roam (otherwise they'd have left Castello). *There are tourists a few blocks over*, he wanted to tell them—*rubes for your angelic faces*. Although he pointed in various directions, he couldn't think how to make the dogs best understand, and they just cocked their heads and stared. Yet for the most part they remained remarkably calm, and why not? They were liberated and free. They stood in stark contrast to New York City dogs, who never stopped to be admired, keeping at all times a frenetic pace, as if the only safety were the interior of a Park Avenue apartment. Particularly Upper East Side dogs, overbred for status-obsessed owners and emotionally wrecked by having to exist on an island with millions of people, all equally high-strung.

He wondered if that was just it; he was a New York dog, while most everyone he'd met, including Darren (despite being from Ohio), was more European. Paul himself would cop to a nervousness that he could never let go of, egged on by New York's relentless pace. Perhaps that was why he was always so desperate to commit. He remembered a confrontation with Darren that was typical of their relationship. They were in Lincoln Square one evening, trying to decide on a movie.

"What about that one at seven fifteen?" Paul pointed up at the marquee. "It has Diane Keaton." He wondered, *How bad could it be?*

"She plays a cheerleader," Darren scoffed.

"That's why it sounds fun."

"At her age it doesn't make sense. She's practically arthritic!"

"They *all* play cheerleaders, that's the point. It's about a squad of retirees." Paul had done his best to sound optimistic. Even a bad movie would get them off the streets and into the air-conditioning, where he could enjoy the darkness and a box of Junior Mints. But he knew that to lure Darren, he would have to sell it just right.

"Let's walk around," Darren had countered. "Maybe we'll

stumble on something better to do." The way he said it, it almost seemed that simple, even though Paul knew how the evening would play out. They'd walk around until they got tired or sweaty, then grab takeout, something familiar, maybe Vietnamese, and the food would be all wrong for their moods. Eventually, Paul would go to bed frustrated, knowing what Darren and others did not: It was rare for something better to come by. Perhaps that's what Darren was doing right now, stumbling around, hoping to find some*one* better to do. He tried not to grow angry thinking about it. Darren was his past, the Dog his future, and as a solo traveler—a *solivagant*—Paul no longer had anyone stopping him from doing as he pleased. He redoubled his search for the Dog.

He moved on to Via Giuseppe Garibaldi, one of Venice's rare wide streets, and successfully ordered an Americano—at last—and sat at a little café table to watch the bustle go by. He saw several more dogs, none his. Perhaps the Dog was too smart to linger among the locals, knowing he'd never encounter more than a sour face taunting him with steamed milk. Feeling newly alive after his coffee, or at least adjacent to human again, Paul made his way back to the loft to fetch his guidebook and the things he would need for his day.

Of course, there in the courtyard was Mama Celeste, this time standing with a much younger woman instead of her broom. "*Mia figlia*," she said, even though Paul was in no mood.

"I feel you, too," he replied, forcing a convivial laugh. Only the younger woman smiled.

"Dott-terr," said Mama Celeste, frustrated not to be understood.

"*Mia figlia* means 'my daughter,'" the younger woman offered in heavily accented but perfect English. She was much taller than her mother, with long, chestnut hair, and wore a polka-dot dress right out of the 1940s that was also very much of today. "I'm Carmolita's daughter."

Paul was about to ask who Carmolita was, but it became instantly clear when Mama Celeste impatiently shoved her daughter forward. She took a few playful steps toward Paul, resting one hand on his chest. "Mama!" she scolded with coquettish embarrassment before offering her hand to Paul. "I'm Sofia," she said with a soft purr, much more Loren than Petrillo.

"Oh, no," Paul said as it dawned on him what was happening.

"*Divorzio!*" Carmolita declared, about him or Sofia he wasn't sure, but he imagined it had to be both.

"Mama," Sofia chided, her face turning bright pink. "I'm sorry, she's very old-fashioned. Her views on men and women are . . ." She grasped for the right word, turning back to her mother as if the answer would be written across her face. And in a manner of speaking it was.

This can't be happening. Paul wondered why he couldn't be struck with the hiccups now. He looked around for the Dog, hoping he would burst into the courtyard, causing Carmolita to reach for her broom, allowing him to escape in the chaos. But he was trapped.

"I have the day free, my mother thought I might show you around," Sofia explained, adjusting his scarf, the very one Nicola had complimented the night prior. "Don't worry, I'm not like my mother. But I understand we have a few things in common."

Like an insatiable lust for men, Paul thought, stopping himself just before he could say it out loud.

"Have you taken a ride in a gondola yet?"

"I—I haven't," Paul confessed, damning himself for not saying he had. But a meal in a restaurant was one thing; a gondola ride alone was out of the question.

"Very romantic, especially this time of year. I know the best gondolier. No one should be alone for Christmas."

There wasn't enough espresso in all of Italy to give Paul the strength to deal with this.

Carmolita clasped her hands together, delighted with the match. "Go! Go!" she shouted, apparently familiar with some English. Paul was so thoroughly convinced she might grab her broom and shoo *them* from the courtyard, he pulled his phone from his pocket and answered it.

"Hello?"

"*Il suo telefono,*" Carmolita exclaimed, reverting back to Italian.

"What's that?" Paul asked, cupping his hand over the speaker, as if placing his nonexistent caller on hold.

"Your phone didn't ring," Sofia declared.

"It's on silent."

"The screen is blank."

Paul looked at his phone, which betrayed him. "Oh. I'm feeling vibrations."

Sofia whispered in his ear. "You feel them, too?" She placed her hands on his shoulders, smoothing the collar on his coat. "May I straighten your collar?"

"Yes, but that's about *all* you can straighten." He looked deep in her brown eyes and held her gaze, making a silent, desperate appeal. If she was indeed more modern than her mother, she must understand, even if his wordplay was lost in translation.

"Oh," she finally said as the reality of their situation dawned on her. "*Sì*. I didn't know. My apologies." She glanced back over her shoulder. "My mother is going to be crushed."

Carmolita turned to her daughter. "*Che cosa?*"

"He's not ready, Mama. It's too soon." She said this in English for Paul's benefit, then repeated herself in Italian.

"*Grazie,*" Paul mouthed to Sofia, who nodded and smiled

in return. Her cheeks were slightly flushed; Paul imagined his were, too. He hastily excused himself, fishing in his pocket for his key. He opened his door and scurried inside, locking all three locks behind him. He pressed his ear to the door and listened to animated bickering in Italian before slinking deeper inside the loft.

Paul woke from a nap and escaped only when he was certain the coast was clear. Last night's dinner was a distant memory and hunger was now settling in. The leftover lasagna he had saved would only make him think of Nicola, so Paul found a moored boat selling produce and purchased a few clementines. He spotted a quiet doorway in which to sit and peeled one of them for a snack. His phone buzzed, startling him; he had begun to feel unreachable and liked being untethered from the outside world. It was an email from Amazon, confirming a package had shipped—Darren buying things still on their joint Prime account. Paul wanted more than anything to click through to the order, to see what Darren had bought for his new life without him, but reasoned no good could come from it (at least without the fortification of a stiff drink). But with the disaster of the morning and the Dog nowhere in sight, his resolve was short-lived, and after finishing two clementines he clicked the link in the email. A stainless steel bread maker boasting three pan sizes and crust settings was somewhere in New York on the back of a truck. *That sonofabitch.* They'd had a sourdough starter a few years back, like many did during that dark year; it fizzled—Darren's interest had been threadbare. But his new life apparently would rise from a foundation of yeast and other ingredients; the bread maker even had a dispenser for fruits and nuts. One reviewer called using the machine "a religious experience."

Unbelievable.

He didn't even have a functioning coffee maker and was stuck in a strange land. Now fully fighting rage, Paul pulled out his guidebook and flipped to the pages on San Rocco, as the day now needed some sort of purpose. The Chiesa di San Rocco was the only church in Venice designed as a sacrarium to hold the remains of its titular saint (*It's like the Guggenheim that way*, he thought). He stared absentmindedly at the photos in his book as he peeled a third clementine, the juices running down his fingers and onto the steps. In one afternoon he could visit both the church and the saint himself. The patron saint of dogs and the falsely accused. *Take that, Darren*, who apparently was seeking a religious experience from homemade rosemary boule. Paul, at least, had an actual saint. What did Darren have? A high-speed agitator to make dough. Paul thought it clear who was winning.

The Chiesa di San Rocco had a beautiful marble facade mottled with dark streaks, the front of the church decorated with statues. Carved into the stone above the main entrance was a relief of the saint, propped up by a staff, arm outstretched, healing the victims of plague. Paul stood in the square between the church and the Scuola Grande di San Rocco, letting people mill about him, squinting in an attempt to make it appear that San Rocco was reaching out to him, but gave up when he couldn't get the right angle. The *scuola* was supposedly filled with magnificent paintings, but while open to the public, it was not what he'd come here to see. Instead he weaved in and out of the crowd, trying to peer through their legs in search of four paws, the front two of them white, working a telltale hustle; sadly, everyone stood upright. He waited to feel some special connection, an enlightenment of sorts. He stood in the square for the better part of an hour, and despite the cloudless blue sky and the way the soft afternoon sunlight made the church's marble glow pink and the sound of Italian words melting together in verse, nothing like that ever came. In a last-ditch effort he entered the church and lit a candle at the altar. Paul had never been much for prayer, but he'd also never been inside a church as ornate as this, with an actual saint interred; that had to count for something. He made his silent wish as he looked up at the stunning paintings that lined the ceilings and arches, men bowing before an all-powerful god. *Please send the Dog my way.* He then laughed, wondering if this god would answer the prayer as asked or assume that Paul was dyslexic.

Discouraged and ready to call it a day, he skirted the dwindling crowds through a quiet alleyway; as usual, he kept his eyes trained on the ground. He needed a plan for dinner; the clementines by themselves would not do. Empty as he felt, he was also stuffed with self-pity, and he wondered as he often did of late which parts of himself he'd inherited. Did he have himself to blame for his utter distaste for being alone? Or was it his father's fault for leaving when Paul was a child, or his mother's for having immediately remarried? Whose history could he claim, whose was he burdened by? Everyone's? Even the earliest humans formed tribes. Or was the answer *no one's*? This train of thought was one more in which he was totally alone.

Paul didn't know exactly what made him glance up when he did; something stirred from deep within. Just ahead, where the alleyway opened onto a small piazza, he spotted the Dog sitting in a halo of light. He sat by himself, his weight on his haunches, listening to choral singers perform baroque music at the open door of a small chapel. The voices were elegiac, beautiful, ricocheting off the buildings on all sides of the piazza, enveloping them in music. The song, Handel's *Messiah*, his mother would play every Christmas for him and his brother; with every *Hallelujah!* the choir's voices vibrated on his skin, making his arm hairs stand on end. Or maybe it was the excitement of finding the Dog, its own miracle, his own prayer answered, that made his heart stand still. Either way, Paul crouched slowly before the open chapel, careful not to get too close; it was finally just the two of them, and he didn't want their meeting to end before it began. The Dog licked his chops and sat, shifting his balance from one paw to the other, uncertain what to make of this moment. Together they listened, the Dog inching toward the door and sitting again, howling occasionally to add his voice to the choir.

Confident he'd earned the Dog's trust, at least enough not to spook him, Paul approached the chapel. A cool draft blew through the stone doorway; he already knew in future retellings he would describe this moment as haunting. "I want to be just like you," he whispered to the Dog, scanning the piazza to see if others could hear. Everything around them was still. "I admire you," he added, reaching into his pocket for cheese. "Your utter comfort being on your own. *Here.*" The Dog sniffed his fingers and accepted the cube of cheese. Paul immediately regretted too easily offering his reward. He spoke again quickly, fearing the Dog would have his fill of him. "I was hoping you'd teach me your secrets. But now that I say that out loud it sounds silly." Sillier still, it occurred to Paul that even if the Dog understood human words, he was used to hearing Italian. "*Segreti?* Secrets."

The Dog refused to tear his eyes from the chapel and cocked his head, confused.

"My heart hurts all the time and I want it not to. *Hurt.* And my brain works overtime. How do you do it? How do you find so much confidence, total peace, in being alone?" Despite the music and the strange circumstances of their meeting, Paul held the Dog's attention. "It's my last night in Venice. I'm leaving tomorrow to go back to New York. I came here with nothing, desperately wanting to leave with *something.* Some small bit of wisdom that might once again fill life with joy. And somehow I've fixated on you as the teacher. *Professore? Sì?* Convinced myself that you know the way. But I don't know that I'm built like you. I don't know that I could be your pupil."

The Dog spun in circles, chasing his tail until he caught the tip, and gnawed at the last wisp of fur. Paul tried to divine a bit of wisdom, something about making ends meet, before he was interrupted by voices from the alley. He turned, but fortune smiled and they headed the opposite way. He looked around at the stone walls that boxed him in. They looked wet in the way Venice was always damp, even though it hadn't rained at all during his stay. The building across from the chapel had two north-facing windows adorned with Christmas wreaths. With their shutters closed and their flower boxes empty, they looked like eyes that were sleeping. Another wall had faded tiles with a pattern that made it look stained with tears. The setting sun barely kissed the rooftops and the square had a Christmas tree covered in angels who, while beautiful, were frozen without a message. All of it so lonely, so void of life, except for his Dog and the music. Paul started to cry.

And then, the Dog let go of his tail and cried, too. Whimpered right alongside him.

It washed over Paul, how silly he'd been. The Dog wasn't any more comfortable alone than he was; he was just used to it, accepting that people behaved in ways that let you down. It was *their* nature. Here, faced with a stranger and something he couldn't explain, the Dog, too, was afraid. But he stayed anyhow to experience it. Perhaps how to be alone wasn't even the lesson Paul was seeking; how to be *present* was. There was music and wonder in life to be had, and yes, sometimes it was nice to experience it with another, but it didn't *come* from being with someone else. The world could be appreciated alone, even when it felt scary. *Does this scare you?* Nicola had asked. In this moment, Paul could honestly say that it didn't. He scratched the Dog behind his ears; his fur was both wiry and soft. Paul offered him a second cube of cheese and the Dog bowed as he chewed, doing that waggish head-down eyes-up thing that had made George Clooney a star. The Dog swallowed, then offered his paw—a gesture of thanks? Or goodbye? Paul started crying harder. He accepted the handshake, cupping the paw in his palms. The Dog made meaningful eye contact, as if telepathic, holding Paul's attention until he turned his gaze back to the chapel. Dazed, Paul barely noticed when the Dog pulled his paw free, trotting away from him down the alley. When it dawned on him what was happening, Paul didn't look. He couldn't bear to see him go.

Paul remained crouched for a time; he wasn't sure how long—seconds, minutes, as long as it took to gather the strength to stand. The choir finished their hymn and began a second, the tempo brisker this time, a lone voice singing a Vivaldi-like aria, the song less solemn, the effect more operatic. Paul turned to face the small church while removing his cap, then wiped the tears from his face. He stepped forward slowly, approaching the entrance with reverence until he was close enough to stick his head through the door. The air inside was even cooler than the winter dusk, and it moved, ever so slightly, around him, as if circulated by a weak fan. The chapel was empty, lit mostly by candles; there was no center aisle and only six rows of pews. None of the paintings that made the Chiesa di San Rocco so ornate. And no choir. No soloist. Where were the singers? Where were these angelic voices coming from? He stood dumbfounded until, just to the left of the door, a faint glint of light caught his attention and Paul strained his eyes to see. *It couldn't be,* he thought, but it was: an old iPod plugged into speakers.

Fraud. It was fraudulent, all of it. The most genuine connection of his trip facilitated by trickery. Paul backed out of the doorway, stunned, speechless, as if he'd seen a ghost. No wonder the Dog had stopped in his tracks; he knew this wasn't right, either. Modernity had no place in a setting like this (although an iPod was decidedly ancient). And artifice had cheapened this moment. And yet when confronted with both he hadn't recognized them until they were staring him in the face. More so, he was *moved* by them—he was still on the verge of tears.

But instead of tears came laughter. Paul burst into uncontrollable giggles that emanated deep from within, the kind of laugh that was cleansing. His marriage, his inability to be alone, the Dog, the espresso machine, Nicola, Nicola's girlfriend, Sofia, his search for meaning. All of it seemed . . . *silly.* He listened as his laughter reverberated around the piazza, replacing the music from the iPod; eventually he had to cup his hands over his face to control himself. When he was finally able to collect his breath, he shoved his hands into his pockets and they squished the last of the cheese, and then the very idea of his carrying cheese in his pocket was funny, rolled in lint as it must have been, and he started laughing again until he was most of the way back to his loft.

Paul lay in the bed where Nicola had been, his shoes dangling off the edge of the mattress. He could still smell the faint whiff of cigarettes on his bedsheets, which would have annoyed him in New York but seemed romantic in Europe; it actually brought him some comfort. He wasn't entirely alone, even when he was—there were echoes of people all around him. *Lo scorpione. His nature.* Paul still didn't know what Nicola had meant, exactly. Was he bisexual? A sex addict? A liar? Maybe it wasn't important for him to know. Still, Paul wondered, between the two of them, who was really the tourist? Perhaps he was more capable of being alone than he thought. At least, in any given place, he knew someone. *Himself.* And that was a real Christmas gift.

On a whim he opened his web browser and searched *New York City Animal Rescue* to look at photos of dogs. A few clicks and his screen filled with one sad face after another. He scrolled through organizations, scanning their pleas for help. Sad dogs, mean dogs, injured dogs, ugly dogs. Volunteer.

Spread the word. Get involved. Donate. Bingo night! Auction! Raffle tickets! WIN! WIN! WIN! It was all overwhelming for his final night in Italy; he should have been researching where to eat, what kind of pasta to enjoy for a last meal before returning to a country that feared gluten. He chastised himself for falling back on old habits, as if already he were devising a way not to be alone when he returned to New York. But something in him—laziness, exhaustion, depletion, ennui—kept him scrolling until he stumbled on something he didn't know he was still looking for in earnest: *a sign*. Like the markers that led to Piazza San Marco and ultimately his way back to the loft, a name jumped out at him as if to light his way home: *Rocco*.

A dog named Rocco. Paul carefully thumbed through the photos on his screen. The dog was blond, almost shockingly so, and only had one eye. His nose was black, as was his wry smile, which seemed to tilt ever just so to one side. In the photos he wore a bandana, which gave him an air of sophistication, a look Paul himself had tried to emulate by purchasing the scarf; in that way they were simpatico. The accompanying text described a friendly dog with a crippling case of separation anxiety and suggested Rocco would do best with someone who worked at home. Paul worked from home two days a week, and his office allowed dogs. Surely that would make him a good fit. Rocco's desire for companionship wasn't a defect, and Paul felt it shouldn't be advertised as such; in fact, to him it was an asset. He looked at his watch. In New York, it was still late afternoon. He stared at the photo of Rocco, and back at his watch, then back at Rocco again. He kicked off his shoes to get comfortable, then sat up to compose an email.

He must have dozed off soon after, as he was startled awake at midnight, the bells of the Piazza San Marco ringing joyously as they echoed through the city announcing the start of Christmas mass. He sat up to listen. He'd imagined Christmas this year would land with a thud, but here it was being heralded with such beauty, and he was reminded of the miracles and renewal the holidays bring.

The sun rose on Christmas morning, casting its familiar light across the loft. In the open kitchen, Paul packed the double-shot filter with rich grounds, an attempt at one last cappuccino, inhaling deeply to rouse himself; he even thought about brushing some grinds on his gums like he once did with a little cocaine at a college party—it might be the closest to caffeine he got.

A loud knock brought him back to his senses and he tiptoed to the door to whisper, "*Buongiorno?*"

A woman replied in Italian. Against his better judgment

he opened the door to reveal his favorite mother-daughter duo. Carmolita, the sturdier of the two, was holding a large box but was quickly buckling under its weight. Paul sprang forward to relieve her of it.

"Allow me." He awkwardly took hold of the package, doing his best to avoid touching her breast. "Where does this go?" he asked, confused as to what to do next.

"*Cucina*," Carmolita barked, in a way that made him think of the Dog.

"It's an espresso machine," Sofia explained. "My mother says the one in this unit has been acting up."

Paul brightened. A true holiday miracle. He was perfectly capable of performing simple tasks for himself—it was the machine that was faulty, not him. "*Buon Natale*," he said. Merry Christmas.

"*Buon Natale*," Carmolita replied, impressed, for once, with his Italian. She then slid a man's wristwatch off her arm and offered it to Paul. It was old, but very handsome.

"What's this?" he asked, confused.

"It was my father's," Sofia explained. "My mother would like you to have it."

Carmolita thrust it forward, closer and closer to his hand.

"Oh. That's very kind, but I couldn't possibly . . ."

Carmolita addressed her daughter, then waited for her to translate.

"She says, 'Time only moves forward.' After my father died, she would look at his watch and understand there was no going back. Now she wants you to do the same."

"But—this should be yours."

Sofia smiled. "I have many things of my father's. All I could ever need."

Losing patience, Carmolita grabbed Paul's hand and shoved the watch into his palm, closing his fingers around it. Stunned, he slid the watch over his fist, the gold band a near perfect fit. The face was simple and displayed only two numbers, twelve and six, the brand Panerai, classic, not fussy. Sure enough, the second hand only ticked forward. Paul watched in a trance as it rotated halfway around the face.

"*Grazie*," he said, his eyes filled with tears.

"*Buon Natale*," Carmolita said again.

"*Buon Natale*," Paul replied. *Time only moves forward.*

The two women stayed only long enough to unbox and set up the machine. Paul asked them to stay now that he could properly entertain, but they begged off for church, Sofia lingering just long enough to blow him a friendly kiss.

Alone, he packed the new filter with grounds and added milk to the machine to froth. He served himself what was left of the panettone, microwaving it under a damp paper towel to soften it. As he waited for his coffee to finally brew, he cleaned out the fridge, tossing the bites of lasagna and the uneaten cheese and dumping the last of the wine. He took his breakfast to the window, pulling aside the gauzy drapes. The Dog was not there, but then Paul hadn't expected him to be. Not this morning. The Dog was no longer his, and had never been to begin with. He was no doubt off panhandling the new arrivals coming to celebrate the new year, perhaps capturing the imagination of someone else disembarking into the city.

He pulled his phone from the charger and spotted two missed texts from Darren.

I was up all night moving the last of my stuff. I'll come back to clean, just need a few hours to rest.

Have a safe flight home.

Paul stared at the screen, feeling numb. And then he glanced at his new watch and it hit him—why did he have to go home? Progress had been made, but there was more work to be done. And it could only be done if he stayed present in *this* moment, answering only to his whims. Time only moves forward. So he texted back.

No rush. I've decided to spend a few days in Berlin.

He had no idea what had made him write that, other than the fact that the in-flight magazine on the plane had listed it as a top city for solo travelers; it had a high score on what they had coined the Happiness Scale. Traveling alone had pushed him outside his comfort zone, but it had also pushed him outside the zone of Darren's expectations of him, and he couldn't help but smile, imagining his ex reacting to his announcement. As soon as he hit send he knew it was exactly what he wanted to do. He called the airline to change his flight, then wrote a heartfelt thank-you note to his hosts.

When his new watch read eleven thirty, he said goodbye to the apartment, dropped the keys in Carmolita's mailbox as instructed, and walked over to a larger canal to meet his water taxi. As he waited, he took everything in one last time, pondering how you ever leave a city like this. (*You don't,* he realized. *You leave with a bit of it inside you.*) When his taxi arrived, he handed the boat captain his suitcase and settled in the stern. As they navigated slowly back down the canal, Paul returned a friendly wave from a woman ashore, then he watched the city recede in the distance as they picked up speed in the bay. Venice had been built as a trading city, a place for commerce, especially for silk and for spice—the world's first true international financial center. But while he was there, Paul had traded in other commodities: self-doubt for self-confidence, heartbreak for renewal, an old love for a new sense of self. He watched as a curious gull flew alongside him, pacing the boat until it had no choice but to land on a pylon to rest. As he sped toward the airport, Paul made the last bargain of his visit to Venice: He would never need anyone again, unless they were open to needing him, too. The world was full of wonders to experience and he, alone, was enough to discover them.

ACKNOWLEDGMENTS

While solo travel can be a life-affirming experience, this particular journey to Venice was taken with many companions. Thank you to my agent, Rob Weisbach, who is up for any adventure. My editor, Kate Dresser, is an absolute joy, and I'm lucky that this is but our maiden voyage. I adore my entire team at G. P. Putnam's Sons. I would go anywhere with you. Especially Tarini Sipahimalani, who stepped in to oversee crucial parts of this excursion. I'm thankful for my dogs past and present: Lily, Tilda, Raindrop, and Shirley. Even though some of you have moved on to your next journeys, I still carry everything I learned from you. And I'm grateful for Byron Lane, my forever travel companion, who never judges the horrible things I eat in airports (*vacation rules* . . . it's a thing) or posts the ridiculous photos he takes of me sleeping on planes. Except that one time.

Lastly, I'm grateful for Italy and the incredible Italian people for welcoming me back to their beautiful country again and again and again. *Ti amo.* I'm overdue for a visit.

ABOUT THE AUTHOR

Author photograph by Afonso Salcedo

Steven Rowley is the *New York Times* bestselling author of *Lily and the Octopus*, a *Washington Post* Notable Book; *The Editor*, an NPR Best Book of the Year; *The Guncle*, winner of the twenty-second Thurber Prize for American Humor and a Goodreads Choice Awards finalist for Novel of the Year; *The Celebrants*, a *Today* show Read with Jenna book club pick; and *The Guncle Abroad*. His fiction has been translated into twenty languages. He resides in Palm Springs, California.

stevenrowley.com

MrStevenRowley